miffy outdoors

This book belongs to:

....

miffy's garden

Miffy loves playing in the garden. She likes to help
Mummy Bunny grow pretty daisies and yummy vegetables,
especially carrots. Add Miffy, some flowers and carrots to create
a garden scene below. What are your favourite things to grow?

miffy at the zoo

Grandfather Bunny and Miffy are visiting the zoo. There are
lots of different animals to see. Do you want to add Miffy,
an elephant, some tortoises and a pair of parrots to the picture?
What is your favourite animal?

miffy at the seaside

Miffy is at the beach today with Boris. They are going to play in the water and build sandcastles. Have you been to the beach before? Use your stickers of Miffy, a sailboat, a beach ball, a spade and some seashells to complete this sunshiny scene.

miffy at the park

Miffy has a new bike! She is cycling through the park to feed the ducks. Add Miffy, some more ducks and some flowers to create a park scene below. Do you like going to the park? What do you think Miffy should feed the ducks?

miffy goes camping

Miffy's daddy and mummy have taken Miffy camping. Miffy is excited to sleep outdoors and she loves her little yellow tent. Would you like to go camping? Use your stickers of Miffy in her tent, the moon and a campfire to complete the picture.

miffy at the farm

Today, Miffy's class is visiting a farm to see where animals live.
Find the stickers of Miffy and her classmates,
a pig and a sheep, and add them to the farm scene.
What animals do you think live on a farm?

the playground

Miffy is at the playground with her friends Boris and Barbara.
Miffy is trampolining! What do you like to play on when you go
to the playground? Add Miffy and Barbara to the playground scene.

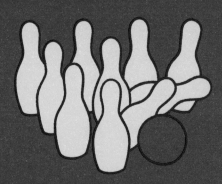

so much fun!

Miffy loves playing outdoors. What do you like to play when you're outside? Put a star sticker next to the picture that you like best. You can go back to the scenes you've created and make up a Miffy story about each one.

see you soon!